FOX AND SQUIRREL
MAKE A FRIEND

Ruth Ohi

Just for Anni and Lex! ♡

♡ Ruth Ohi

North Winds Press
An Imprint of Scholastic Canada Ltd.

www.scholastic.ca

Library and Archives Canada Cataloguing in Publication
Ohi, Ruth, author
Fox and Squirrel make a friend / Ruth Ohi.
ISBN 978-1-4431-3320-3 (bound)
I. Title.
PS8579.H47F696 2014   jC813'.6   C2014-901803-7

Author photo by Annie T.

6 5 4 3 2 1   Printed in Malaysia   108   14 15 16 17 18

For Ian

Squirrel loved the
tops of trees.

"Come and see what I see,"
said Squirrel.

"Okay," said Fox.

6

"Maybe start smaller," said Squirrel.

So Fox tried smaller.

"This is exciting," said Fox.

Boing!

Boing!

Then **whoosh**

went the wind.

Squirrel landed in a tree.
Fox did not.

"What do you see?" said Fox.

12

"Everything!" said Squirrel.
". . . and something yellow."

13

flap

flap

"I can stand on one foot,"
said Yellow Bird.

"Me, too," said Squirrel.

14

"Me, too!" said Fox
from below.

"I can hop from branch to branch,"
said Yellow Bird.

"Me, too!" said Squirrel.

"Me, too!" said Fox.

hop hop

hop

oof!

"I can swoop and soar," said Yellow Bird.

18

"You swoop well!" said Squirrel,
scrambling back up to Yellow Bird.

Fox swooped.

Fox soared.

flap

flap

"Squirrel does not need me,"
said Fox.

So Fox went home.

Back up in the branches,
Yellow Bird flew.

"I am fast," said Yellow Bird.

"My friend Fox is
fast, too," said Squirrel.

But where was Fox?

"I do not see everything," said Squirrel.
"I do not see Fox."

Squirrel scrambled down and found Fox.

"Fox, this is Yellow Bird," said Squirrel.
"Yellow Bird, this is Fox."

"I hear you are fast,"
said Yellow Bird.

Fox smiled.